SLIME TIME!

by John Sazaklis

illustrated by Patrycja Fabicka

Raintree is an imprint of Capstone Global Library
Limited, a company incorporated in England and
Wales having its registered office at 264 Banbury
Road, Oxford, OX2 7DY – Registered company
number: 6695582

www.raintree.co.uk
myorders@raintree.co.uk

ISBN 978 1 3982 0251 1

Designed by Sarah Bennett
Originated by Capstone Global Library Ltd
Printed and bound in the United Kingdom

Acknowledgements
Shutterstock: ALEXEY GRIGOREV, design element, vavectors, design
element, Zaie, design element

British Library Cataloguing in Publication Data
A full catalogue record for this book is available from the
British Library.

CONTENTS

CHAPTER ONE

SNACK ATTACK

"All aboard! We are about to set sail," the captain announced.

Sam had never been on a cruise ship before.

"I can't wait to explore," she said. "There are twelve decks on this ship, and half of them have food!"

"There will be plenty of time to do that after we settle in," her dad replied.

"There's no way I can wait. The all-you-can-eat buffet has just opened," Sam said. "And I want to eat while I'm still young! See ya!"

Sam squeezed herself into the
dining hall. She zoomed straight
for the pastries. She got a huge jam
doughnut topped with icing.

Sam took the biggest bite she
could and quickly spat it out.

"YUCK!" she cried. "This tastes
like slime!"

"How do you know what slime
tastes like?" a red-haired lady asked.

"How do you *not*?" Sam replied.

Suddenly, the splattered jam on the floor began to move. It reached up and wrapped around Sam's arm and leg.

"Help!" shouted Sam. "The jam is alive, and it's going to eat me!"

CHAPTER TWO
SO. MUCH. SLIME.

"Drop the doughnut!" the lady yelled.

Sam let it go, and the slime slid off her. But then it latched onto the doughnut. Sam watched the jam blob gobble up the doughnut.

The blob grew bigger and bigger and bigger.

"Whoa," Sam said. "And I thought *I* was hungry!"

The blob grew two tentacles out of its gloopy side. Then it started to rise.

Thinking quickly, Sam grabbed another snack and threw it across the room.

"Fetch!" she cried.

Leaving a trail of jammy goo,
the blob slithered towards the treat.
"Run for your lives!" Sam yelled
as she ran out of the room.

The diners ignored her and
continued stuffing their faces.

Suddenly, there
was a loud sound.

HOOOOONK!

Sam thought
the ship was
blowing its horn.
But that was not
it. Instead, it was
a new, bigger blob
blowing her nose.

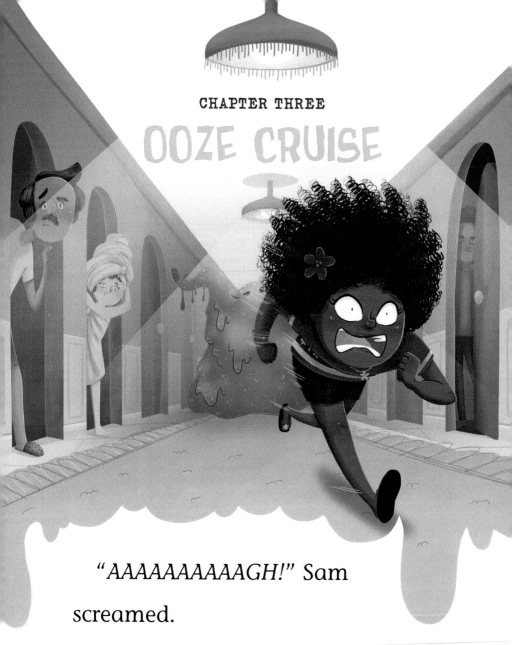

CHAPTER THREE

OOZE CRUISE

"*AAAAAAAAAGH!*" Sam

screamed.

HOOOOOOOOOONK!

The big blob blubbered again.

Sam turned on her heels and ran

in the other direction.

Oh no! The path was blocked by another giant blob.

"I'm surrounded by big, slimy blobs!" Sam shouted.

She was trapped. The only place to go was back to the buffet.

Back at the buffet, Sam was shocked by what she saw.

Piles of food and globs of slime were splattered around a very angry mob.

The original blob was nowhere to be found.

"There's the culprit! This is all her fault!" the red-haired lady shouted, pointing at Sam.

Just then, the room went dark. People screamed. All around them, thick, slimy ooze dripped through the portholes and down the walls.

The ooze slid into the middle of the room and became two separate shapes. The shapes turned into the big blobs Sam had seen in the corridor!

The blobs let out a loud, rumbling sound.

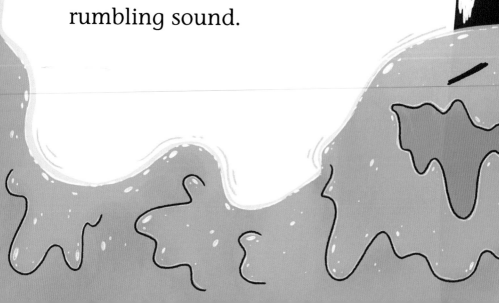

Just then, the original little blob came out from under a table. With a high-pitched squeal, it slithered over to the big blobs.

Their tentacles twisted around each other in a big blob hug.

Sam was still in shock when the
captain entered the dining room.

"Sorry, everyone. These worried
parents were just looking for their
child," she said. "Thankfully
they've found each other!"

The three blobs let out a series of gurgles and burbles.

"How wonderful!" replied the captain. "They've offered to clean up this mess!"

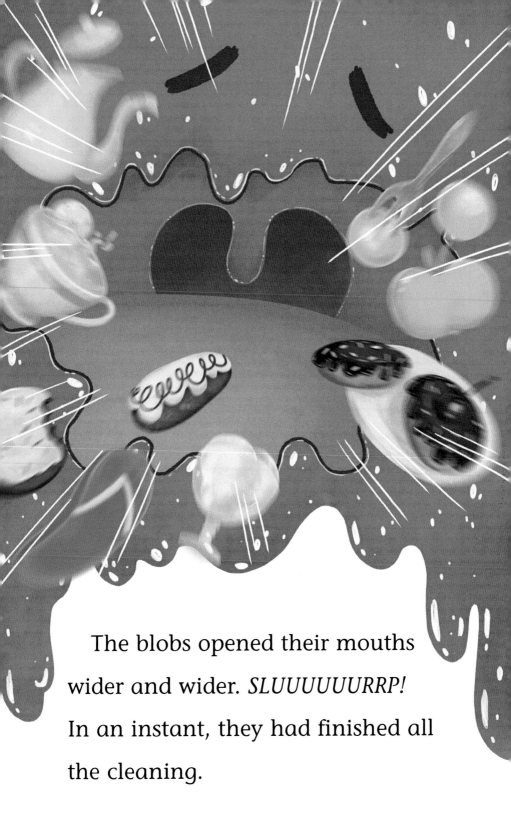

The blobs opened their mouths wider and wider. *SLUUUUUURRP!* In an instant, they had finished all the cleaning.

The blobs belched loudly and oozed out a porthole. At that moment, Sam's dad walked in.

"There you are!" he said. "I'm starving."

Then he looked around. Not only was all the food gone, but so were the cups, plates, napkins, cutlery and the buffet table!

"Wow," said Sam's dad. "When they say 'all-you-can-eat' they really mean it."

"You have no idea!" Sam replied.

AUTHOR

John Sazaklis is a *New York Times* bestselling author with almost 100 children's books under his utility belt! He has also illustrated Spider-Man books, created toys for *MAD* magazine and written for the BEN 10 animated series. John lives in New York City, USA, with his super-powered wife and daughter.

ILLUSTRATOR

Patrycja Fabicka is an illustrator with a love for magic, nature, soft colours and storytelling. Creating cute and colourful illustrations is something that warms her heart – even during cold winter nights. She hopes that her artwork will inspire children, as she was once inspired by *The Snow Queen, Cinderella* and other fairy tales.

blubber to cry loudly

culprit a person who is guilty of doing something wrong

deck the floor of a ship

latch to attach

mob a large group of people

porthole a small, round window in the side of a ship

slither to slip and slide along like a snake

tentacle a long, flexible limb found on some animals

DISCUSSION QUESTIONS

1. Did you think this story was scary, funny or both? Talk about your answer.

2. Why do you think nobody listens to Sam when she tells them to run on page 12?

3. Were you surprised the blobs turned out to be a family? Why or why not?

WRITING PROMPTS

1. The author uses a lot of action words in the story. Make a list of at least five and circle your favourite one.

2. Would you like to go on a cruise? Write a paragraph explaining your answer.

3. Pretend you are Sam. Write a diary entry about your exciting day.

SCARED SILLY
JOKES!

Why couldn't the ship passengers play cards?

Because the captain was standing on the deck.

What did one ocean say to the other ocean when they first met?

Nothing. They just waved.

What kind of ship never sinks?

friendship

What did the baby slime say to its parents?
Goo-goo!

What is slime's favourite game?
Slimon Says

How do you learn more about slime?
You Goooogle it.

What do sea monsters eat?
fish and ships

What did the monster ask his girlfriend on Valentine's Day?
Will you please be my valen-slime?

BOO BOOKS

Discover more just-right frights!

Only from Raintree